SEEDS

BEST QUALITY

Mixed Boys & Girls

For Greg, Naomi, Théo, and Sebastian

Copyright © 2005 by Belinda Downes

All rights reserved.

First U.S. edition 2006

Library of Congress Cataloging-in-Publication Data is available.

Library of Congress Catalog Card Number 2004065951

ISBN 0-7636-2786-0

2 4 6 8 10 9 7 5 3 1

Printed in China

This book was typeset in p22 Folk Art Cross and Gararond.
The illustrations were done in embroidery, appliqué, and watercolor.

Candlewick Press

2067 Massachusetts Avenue

Cambridge, Massachusetts 02140

visit us at www.candlewick.com

BABY DAYS

A Quilt of Rhymes and Pictures

BELINDA DOWNES

CANDLEWICK PRESS
CAMBRIDGE, MASSACHUSETTS

WISHING FOR A BABY

Star light, star bright,
First star I see tonight,

I wish I may, I wish I might,
Have the wish I wish tonight.

WELCOME TO YOUR HOME

log cabin

cottage

apartment building

palace

skyscraper

mansion

hut

lighthouse

houseboat

trailer

castle

tree house

tower

igloo

Which home do you like best?

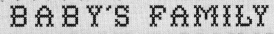

'Neath the spreading chestnut tree, I loved you and you loved me.
There you'd sit upon my knee, 'neath the spreading chestnut tree.

babies   mothers   fathers   brothers   sisters

'Neath the spreading chestnut tree, there you said you'd marry me.
Now you should see our family, 'neath the spreading chestnut tree.

uncles   aunts   cousins   grandmas   grandpas

THE BIG WIDE WORLD

I saw a ship a-sailing,
A-sailing on the sea,
And oh, but it was laden
With pretty things for thee.

The captain was a duck
With a packet on his back.
And when the ship began to move,
The captain said, "Quack! Quack!"

What can you see in the big wide world?

BABY'S CLOTHES

overalls

skirt

sweater

undershirt

scarf

shoes

mittens

shorts

hat

boots

pants

tights

dress

What shall we wear today?

BABY'S FACES

thoughtful	curious	plane-watching	teething	needy

happy	quiet	surprised	sneaky	planning

angry	puzzled	lovable	waving	sleeping

HEAD, SHOULDERS,

Head, shoulders, knees, and toes,
Head, shoulders, knees, and toes,
And eyes and ears and mouth and nose,
Head, shoulders, knees, and toes.

KNEES & TOES

MEALTIME

bottle-fed

slice of
melon

bowl of
cereal

plate of
sandwiches

fruit

dairy

grain

Jelly on the plate,
Jelly on the plate,

Wibble, wobble, wibble, wobble,
Jelly on the plate.

vegetable purée

hamburger and hot dogs

bowl of ice cream

breast-fed

vegetables

cakes

desserts

Baby on the floor,
Baby on the floor,

Pick him up, pick him up,
Baby on the floor.

BATH TIME

Charlie, Charlie in the tub,
Charlie, Charlie pulled the plug.
Oh my goodness, oh my soul,
There goes Charlie down the hole!

duck

toothbrushes

sponge

powder

cotton balls

towel

wash-cloth

soap

hairbrush

comb

pitcher

shampoo and conditioner

shells

boat

Rubber ducks and other things

BABY'S ROOM

Five little monkeys jumping on the bed,
One fell off and bumped his head.
Mommy called the doctor, and the doctor said,
"No more monkeys jumping on the bed!"

Which is your favorite toy?

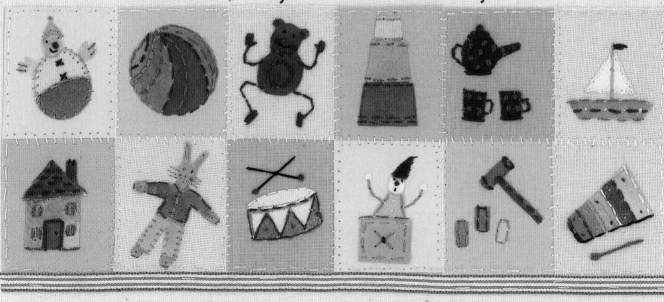

DANCING and SINGING

Dance to your daddy,
My little laddie.
Dance to your daddy,
My little lamb!

You shall have a fishy
In a little dishy.
You shall have a fishy
When the boat comes in.

I sing, I sing,
From morn till night;
From cares I'm free,
And my heart is light.

Rock-a-bye, baby, on the treetop.
When the wind blows, the cradle will rock.
When the bough breaks, the cradle will fall,
And down will come baby, cradle and all.

BEDTIME

Golden slumbers kiss your eyes;
Smiles awake you when you rise.
Sleep, pretty wantons, do not cry,
And I will sing a lullaby:
Rock them, rock them, lullaby.

Care is heavy, therefore sleep you;
You are care and care must keep you.
Sleep, pretty wantons, do not cry,
And I will sing a lullaby:
Rock them, rock them, lullaby.

Good night.

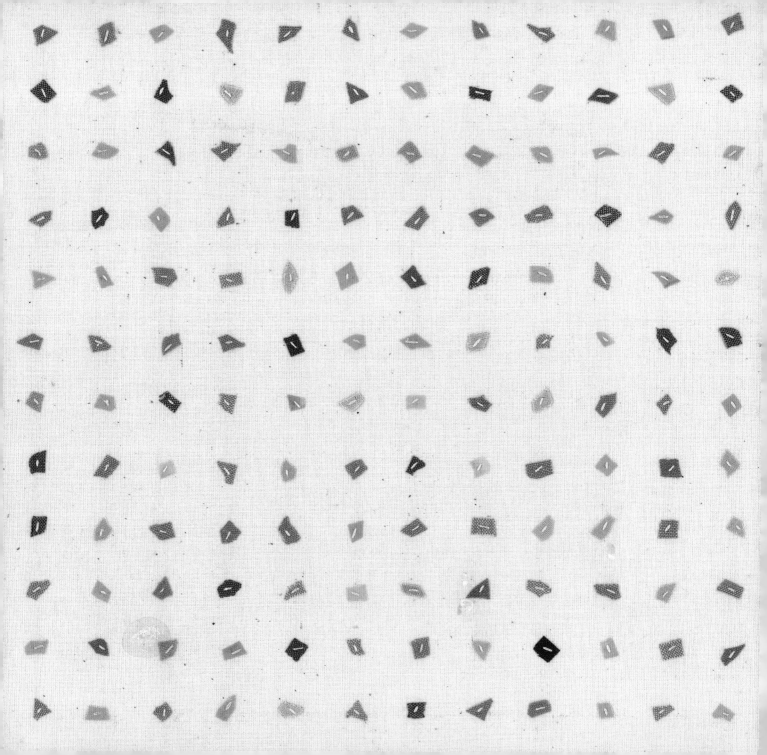